The Riddle of Changewater Pond

by Margaret C. Cooper

Bradbury Press • *New York*

Maxwell Macmillan Canada • Toronto
Maxwell Macmillan International
New York • Oxford • Singapore • Sydney

Bradbury Press
Macmillan Publishing Company
866 Third Avenue
New York, NY 10022

Maxwell Macmillan Canada, Inc.
1200 Eglinton Avenue East
Suite 200
Don Mills, Ontario M3C 3N1

Macmillan Publishing Company is part of the Maxwell Communication Group of Companies.

First edition
Printed and bound in the United States of America
10 9 8 7 6 5 4 3 2 1

The text of this book is set in 14-point Galliard.

Library of Congress Cataloging-in-Publication Data
Cooper, Margaret C.
    The riddle of Changewater Pond / by Margaret C. Cooper.—1st ed.
        p.   cm.
    Summary: While in eleven-year-old Kevin's care, Aunt Fiona's prize Irish setter is transformed into a human boy after a swim in a magical pond.
    ISBN 0-02-724495-4
    [1. Dogs—Fiction.   2. Magic—Fiction.]   I. Title.
PZ7.C78736Ri   1993
[Fic]—dc20   93-15699

To my sister, Carol

1

Kevin Mason deftly kicked a hightop sneaker across the floor and under his bed. He couldn't find the other one anyway, so what use was it? He scooped an armful of crumpled clothing from his bed and a jumble of Fantastix comic books, a squashed banana peel, and three lucky wishbones off his desk, then crammed everything into the bottom of his closet.

He was really glad that his aunt from Ireland was coming to visit. She was fun. But

1

why should *his* bedroom have to be so grossly neat? After all, Aunt Fiona and her Irish setter would be staying in the downstairs room. At the thought of the dog, Kevin sighed. It wasn't that he didn't like dogs. But, well, some of those Irish setters were kind of big.

As if on cue, a silver station wagon with a rental license plate crunched to a stop in the driveway beneath Kevin's window. He ran for the stairs.

A moment later, Kevin was surrounded by swirls of rust, red, and brown. Aunt Fiona, her bright hair flying, grabbed him hard and twirled him about the foyer until his head spun. At her side a huge setter pranced and barked as if he considered himself part of the greeting committee.

"Oh, Kevy, Kevy," his aunt gasped at last, holding him at arm's length, "it's so good to have your bones in me clutches again. Why, you've grown to be a great handsome lad since I saw you last. Och, eleven years old already, and with the wavy blond hair that will drive the girls wild."

Kevin blushed, feeling suddenly tongue-tied. Before he could respond, his mother dashed into the room, followed closely by his father. The two sisters flew into each other's arms.

This time, however, Fiona's dog found a way to join the celebration. Tail waving delightedly, he leaped up on Kevin, knocking him backward against the steps. There he began to sluice the boy down with a wet tongue.

"H-hey, Aunt Fiona, call off the troops," cried Kevin. He felt as if he were pinned down by a thirsty grizzly bear.

"Ah, don't mind Tim, love," his aunt called over her sister's shoulder. "Just step on his toes if he jumps up."

Kevin took one look into the set of gleaming teeth so close to his nose and shrank back farther on the step. Was she kidding? He'd sooner kick a land mine to teach it some manners.

Kevin's mother turned and quickly whistled Tim to her side. "Oh, Fiona," she cried, stroking him. "He's just magnificent. What's his kennel name?"

"Haven't I introduced me prize show dog properly then?" With a proud flourish of the arm, Aunt Fiona announced, "Kevin, Kate, John, I'd like you to meet the future canine champion of the world—Tara's Redlightning Timothy!"

Tim's silky tail thumped hard against the floor and his mouth opened in a wide grin. He was so obviously pleased by the attention that even Kevin laughed.

When they sat down to dinner that evening, Tim lay in the doorway, following the lively conversation from person to person as if enjoying the sound of their voices.

Finally Fiona nodded at him. "Okay, Tim, I guess you'll be needin' to stretch your legs outside about now. How about it, Kevin, would you mind taking him into the backyard while we clear the table?"

Kevin shrugged and followed the bounding animal into the securely fenced yard. Once there he wasn't sure what to do with him.

Tim, however, knew exactly what a dog should do. He set out on a thorough investigation of each bush and tree, which he promptly marked as his own. That accomplished, he grabbed a stick from a patch of overgrown grass and dropped it at Kevin's feet. Seeing Kevin hesitate, the big dog crouched playfully with his forelegs splayed apart, his rump in the air, and tail waving.

Kevin grinned. This guy was a real clown. But even as he bent to pick up the stick, he saw the fur along Tim's spine bristle. He yanked his hand back. Then, following the direction of Tim's gaze, he saw the gray cat from next door gliding like a shadow among his mother's forsythia bushes.

A rush of fury brought Kevin upright. Just yesterday that cat had snatched a baby robin from its nest in the Masons' shrubs. "Get out of here, Tiger!" he shouted. "Stay in your own yard, you rotten cat!"

Responding instantly to the anger in Kevin's voice, Tim shot forward, snarling. The cat leaped frantically for the fence. It fled along the top board with Tim following below, barking and snapping his teeth with evident enjoyment.

Kevin's fists clenched in fierce satisfaction. "Yeah! Way to go, Tim."

From the open kitchen window, Mr. Mason's voice rang out sternly. "Stop that racket, Tim! What are you up to out there?"

Tim halted immediately. Confused, he crept across the grass and pressed his muzzle into Kevin's hand.

Kevin stiffened, and then a tingle of pleasure ran through him. Tim was coming to *him* for refuge. Tentatively he ran his fingers down the dog's long, silky ears. "Hey, no problem, Dad," he called aloud. "Tim and I are just fooling around a little."

"Is that so?" his father retorted. "Well, why don't you try fooling around a little with the lawn mower tomorrow? You're not taking care of your responsibilities, young man!"

Kevin groaned, and Tim moved closer, settling his bony haunch right on Kevin's little toe.

The next morning, after Kevin's parents had gone to work, Aunt Fiona appeared in the kitchen, wearing jeans. After she and Kevin fed Tim his breakfast, she asked, "Want to go with us on a trainin' session, Kevin? We need to keep up Tim's routine, especially at this stage in his development."

"Sure, I'd like that," he said eagerly. He could always cut the grass some other time.

Twenty minutes later they were walking across the village green, where shifting patterns of sunshine and shadow dappled the gravel pathways. "I just love your New England towns," said Kevin's aunt. "They all have these pretty parks with white bandstands and revolutionary war monuments."

"I liked living in the city better," said Kevin. "This little burg has been totally dead since we moved here. I don't know many kids yet, and even Mom goes off to her new job every day. What a great summer—just doing chores and checking in with her by phone a million times a day."

Fiona turned at the note of resentment in

his voice. "This move has been quite a change for you, hasn't it? But you're a big lad, and your mum really loves her real estate job."

Kevin brightened. "Actually, I did meet a guy my age named Richie Owen. We were supposed to go camping out on his farm, but he had to go visit his sick grandmother."

As they crossed the street, they were met by deep-throated barking from within a white frame house. "That's Bridget in there," remarked Kevin. "She's an Irish setter, too. The only other one, crazy old Corky Brown, lives down the street from us. You know, I never gave a thought to the dog population before you two came here."

Aunt Fiona smiled at him. "Well, you're making up for lost time now. Tim is wild about you, Kevin. He's just about your age, you know, in dog years."

Kevin nodded. "Is Tim any good at this obedience stuff, Aunt Fiona?" he asked, "Sometimes he acts like he's still a goofy puppy."

"Sure an' that's one reason why I love him

so," she said, laying a hand lightly on Tim's head as he trotted at her side. "But, Kevy, don't mistake high spirits for stupidity. He's a smart dog, and he's going to be an all-around champion one of these days. Aren't you, boy-o?"

Tim looked at her adoringly and waved a richly plumed tail.

"He sure seems to understand compliments," Kevin said with a grin.

They walked onto a sunny field behind the high school, where an ecstatic Tim set off at full speed across the turf.

Kevin whistled admiringly. "Now I know where you got the 'Redlightning' part of Tim's name. He is *awesome!*"

"Hey, Kevy, you're a man after me own heart," Fiona exclaimed, squeezing his shoulder. "I hope he makes that kind of an impression on a certain young American veterinarian I know. His name's Conor McGuire, and we met back in Ireland, where he was visitin' relatives. Conor seemed seriously interested in my new setup for breedin' and trainin' Irish setters. I hope I can talk him into a partnership when I see him in a few weeks."

Kevin felt like cheering. "Go for it, Aunt Fi! A vet could be the perfect partner for you. Then he must have seen Tim when he was there?"

"Only as a half-grown pup. And before Conor sees him again, I intend to add some American dog show honors to Tim's record. He'll win ribbons in the beauty categories, but we may run into trouble in the obedience trials. Tim has picked up a bad habit lately— well, watch us go through the routine now and tell me what you think."

She whistled shrilly and Tim loped back to her. Flattered at her confidence in him, Kevin never took his eyes from them all the time they were in the field.

The set of exercises ranged from a simple "sit at heel" to walking a tight figure eight with Tim off leash to a maneuver where he had to respond to signals from a distance.

When they finished, Kevin applauded vigorously. "Hooray for the new champ! That was great. Why, half the time Tim was into the next routine before you even gave the command, Aunt Fi."

"Aha, you noticed!" A line of irritation creased his aunt's forehead as she walked Tim off the field. "This young boy-o is too independent. He knows the commands so well that he can guess which will come next. He's not waiting for my body signals to guide him. Somehow I've got to get through to him—fast!"

Sensing her annoyance, the big Irisher backed away a few steps and whined.

Kevin felt sorry for him. "He looked about perfect to me, Aunt Fi. If he knows what to do, why should he wait around?"

Fiona shook her head. "These exercises aren't a game, Kevin. They're designed to teach control and cooperation," she said. "A working dog—a hunter, shepherd, guard, et cetera, *must* accept its handler's guidance or risk makin' dangerous mistakes."

"But Tim really wants to please you, Aunt Fi. And he seems to love doing that stuff."

Kevin smiled at the way Tim was now prancing jauntily at her side as they walked toward home.

When they reached Kevin's backyard, his aunt paused. "I'm glad you came with us today, Kevin," she said. "You're good with Tim and I need your help. I have to fly to North Carolina this weekend and get back before the first dog show. Will you take care of Tim for me then, even though your mum won't be around much to help?"

"Sure I will!" cried Kevin. "Don't worry about a thing, Aunt Fi, I won't let anything happen to him!"

Looking down at Tim, Kevin saw a four-leaf clover growing right between his front feet. A strange excitement traveled up his spine. Wow, just he and Tim alone; what fantastic adventures they could have!

·:3 2 (ε··

On the same evening that Fiona left for North Carolina, Kevin got an unexpected call from Richie Owen.

"Hey, Rich, it's so great that you're back," Kevin said, with his eyes on Tim. "You'll never believe what I have to show you! What're you doing tomorrow?"

"Not much. Come on over. Let's do that overnight camp-out we planned before. Bring the tent and stuff, okay?"

After they hung up, Kevin started downstairs to tell his parents about the camp-out. Midway, he stopped. "Uh-oh, Tim," he whispered to the dog, close behind him. "Mom and Dad will really hassle me big time about taking you camping. I'd better put that off until morning."

But in the morning it was just as bad as he'd expected.

"What? You want to take a valuable dog like Tim tenting in the woods, Kevin?" Mrs. Mason frowned across the breakfast table at her son. "It's enough of a responsibility to care for Tim here at home."

"Aw, c'mon Mom, we're only camping out one night, and we'll be close by in the field behind Richie's house. He's the only friend I have around here, and we've had to postpone this camp-out once already, remember?"

Kevin's father looked up from his newspaper. "What about the grass, Kevin?" he asked sternly. "I've reminded you to cut it several times. The side yard looks particularly unsightly."

Kevin gulped. "It was starting to get dark

out there last night, Dad. And anyway, I thought I'd let it go for a while because . . . because of all those little purple wildflowers growing between the tufts."

Mr. Mason opened his mouth to say more, but Kevin's mother intervened.

"Ah, that's nice, Kev," she said warmly. "I guess you deserve a little fun. And since my sister trusts you to care for her show dog, why shouldn't I? But you'll have to promise to call me so I'll know you're all right."

Kevin agreed, and bolted up the stairs before one of them remembered that he hadn't loaded the dishwasher. As he was stuffing some extra clothes into a backpack, a series of muffled thumps sounded from under the bed.

Smiling, Kevin lifted the corner of the spread. "So, that's where you disappeared to," he whispered. "You can come out now. The fireworks are over."

Tim seemed to get the message, for he edged his way out from under the low bed and wagged his tail.

Outside, a fresh morning breeze was nudging wisps of gray cloud away from the glittering August sun.

Kevin's spirits rose. He stopped by the garage to pick up his camping gear. "We're going to have an absolute blast, Tim—just you and me, and Rich. With no adults around to tell us what to do."

Tim nudged Kevin's hand and rumbled companionably deep in his throat. Kevin loved the way Tim always responded when he was spoken to. Sometimes it was a bright glance or a wag of the tail, but often it was vocal. "He's got more opinions than an Irish politician in a pub," Aunt Fiona had once said. Maybe that was why Kevin had fallen into her way of talking aloud to him.

They turned right at the village green and passed a row of shops and the library. At the edge of town, they followed a narrow tarred road to the top of a rise. There Kevin stopped to shift his tent bag from one shoulder to the other. He surveyed the large clapboard farmhouse below them for signs of life. All was still. Glancing at his watch, he said, "We're kind of early. Let's set up the campsite before we go for Rich. He's going to flip out when he sees you, Tim."

They turned onto a dirt track that led directly into the meadow behind the Owens' barn. There, in the shade of two maple trees, Kevin set up his new tan nylon pop-tent. He filled his air mattress and unrolled the sleeping bag. After placing everything neatly inside the tent, he stepped back to admire his handiwork.

Tim had been following Kevin's every move, sniffing curiously at each item as it appeared. Now, seeing Kevin pause, he pounced on the Frisbee peeping out of the backpack and flirted it invitingly in front of him.

"Okay, boy, let's give it a whirl," Kevin said, smiling. "We're still plenty early."

He grabbed at the Frisbee in the dog's mouth, but Tim twisted his head to the side. With a joyful bark, he galloped out into the open field. Suddenly a large rabbit dashed from the cover of a bush. Dropping the

Frisbee, Tim veered about like a hooked fish and took off after it.

"Hey! Hey Tim, get back here," shouted Kevin. Then, remembering to use the formal command, he called, "Timothy, *come*! Timothy, *come*!" But it was too late. Both dog and rabbit had disappeared into the woods at the edge of the field.

Kevin tore after them in a panic. At first the deep shade blinded him, but he stumbled onward, fending off whiplike birch branches. After several minutes he stopped to call again and to wipe the perspiration out of his eyes. A volley of excited barks sounded from behind a clump of evergreens nearby. There he found Tim, digging furiously at a rabbit burrow between the roots of a pine tree.

"Darn it, Tim!" cried Kevin angrily. "You're supposed to be smart, but here you go acting like a goofball again."

Tim kept right on digging.

"You were *bad*, Tim. What would Aunt Fiona do if anything happened to you?"

At the name Fiona, Tim lifted his head. He

stared at Kevin intently with his ears raised. His dirt-caked nose began to twitch questioningly from side to side.

"Poor guy," Kevin said, pushing down a twinge of jealousy. "You miss her, don't you? C'mon, let's go back. But this time I'm holding tight to your collar."

Going back proved to be more of a problem than he had anticipated. After a hot and frustrating half hour, he realized that they were lost.

Suddenly the shadowed woodland seemed vast, trackless, and mysterious. Rivulets of sweat ran down between Kevin's shoulder blades. Forcing himself to look about calmly, he noticed that the trees to his left were farther apart. He thought he could see sunlight streaming down beyond them. Surely the Owens' open fields lay in that direction.

But when he and Tim finally broke through the last line of trees, he stared in dismay. He had never seen this place before. They were in a grassy clearing overgrown with briers and patches of wild huckleberry bushes. From the rise where a house may once have stood, the ground sloped steeply to a pond. Not a breeze stirred. Not a sound came to their ears.

The nerves at the base of Kevin's neck prickled. He released Tim with a word of warning, and they began to push their way downward through the knee-high grass. Suddenly Kevin's foot struck something and he fell flat on his face.

Pushing aside Tim's anxiously snuffling muzzle, Kevin discovered what he'd tripped over. Hidden in the grass beside him was a decaying wooden sign. He turned it over. "CHANGEWATER POND: WHAT YOU SEE IS WHAT YOU GET. Changewater Pond—is that supposed to be the name of this place? Let's go take a look, Tim."

Tim barked approvingly, and together they bounded down the slope to the banks of the irregularly shaped pond. Bright flecks of sunshine glinted off the surface of brown water. A yellowish vapor hung in the still air above it.

Kevin felt Tim nudge his hand. "I know you're hot, boy," he said, "but I don't think you should swim in that stuff. It smells kind of gross."

Feeling hot and exhausted, Kevin dropped onto a grassy hummock and lay back, closing his eyes. Tim crouched reluctantly beside him.

Something scuttled lightly across Kevin's outstretched hand. Through heavy lids he saw a mud-colored salamander gliding away toward the pond. It slipped into the water, disturbing a small green frog that croaked hollowly from a rock on the bank.

The water in the pond began to churn as if stirred by a huge, invisible spoon. A second green frog clambered hastily out and joined the first on its stony perch.

The swirling waters caught Tim's attention and he whined longingly. He gazed intently at Kevin, then back at the pond.

"Okay, okay, you win," Kevin murmured drowsily. "So go take a swim—I'll hose you off later. Just *come right back!*"

He heard Tim scramble to his feet, and seconds later there was a tremendous splash. Tim must have done a world-record belly flop.

Uh-oh, it's goofball time again, Kevin thought, getting slowly to his feet.

Just as he got to the water's edge, a reddish shape bobbed to the surface. "Hey, Tim," Kevin called, "how ya doing?" Wide-eyed and flailing, Tim gasped and promptly sank again. The entire murky pond seemed to roil and bubble like the brew in a witch's cauldron. Kevin's smile faded. Tim had been underwater for a long time. What was wrong?

Then, amid wild splashing, the dark red thatch reappeared close to shore. To Kevin's dumbfounded amazement, a naked boy almost blinded by a streaming mop of auburn hair crawled onto the bank. He sprawled full length, his lanky form shaken by spasms of violent coughing.

After a quick glance to see that the stranger would survive, Kevin dashed along the bank shouting, "Tim! Tim! Where are you?"

The boy on the grass whimpered, and coughed up more water. Raising his head, he whispered hoarsely, "Here . . . behind ye, K-Kev!"

Kevin spun about, his eyes fastening on the boy's neck. "How did you get that collar? Who are you, and what have you done with my dog?"

At this, the boy's long face wrinkled into an expression of utter confusion. With a strangled yelp he rolled over, staring at himself in horror.

Kevin stared, too, beginning to fear that he was alone in the woods with a raving maniac.

The strange boy rose shakily onto his hands and knees, making peculiar rumbling sounds deep in his throat. After several tries he croaked brokenly, "Och, Kevin Mason . . . sure an' it's a cruel trick . . . you've played on a simple . . . creature like myself. Leavin' me skint naked like some sort of a . . . poor-lookin' pink worm!"

And, twisting his head to peer over his shoulder, he wailed, "Where's me beoo-tiful silky coat . . . and oh, what has become of me pride of a bushy tail?"

3

Gasping, Kevin backed away from the weird redheaded boy blinking in the sunlight. But he couldn't take his eyes from that long, somehow familiar face. "What's g-going on around here?" he stammered. "Where is Tim?"

"I'm here, I tell you. . . ." Abruptly the boy paused and clutched at his throat. "Arrgh-h! Kevin, d'you hear me? I'm . . . I'm *talkin'*!"

But Kevin turned from him in confusion. He dashed along the shoreline peering frantically into the depths of the pond. A ragged call broke from his lips. "Come back, Tim-m-m!"

The other boy had hitched himself closer to the water and was now staring dismally at his reflection. "Ugh, I can't believe the . . . the looks of me either, Kevin," he said falteringly. "But will you listen to the . . . words fallin' from me lips like. . . . They must come along with this, uh, . . . 'man-suit' I'm wearin'."

Kevin's knees trembled. He stuck both fingers in his ears and screwed his eyes shut. NO! This isn't happening! he thought. It's too crazy—I've got to get out of here! But his feet refused to move. Overwhelmed by curiosity, he peered again at the stranger.

Still on his hands and knees, the boy was shaking water off himself by shuddering his body from head to toe. He stopped abruptly, feeling the intensity of Kevin's gaze, and yelped in a rusty-sounding tenor, "C'mon, Kevin . . . enough of this bloody . . . er . . . fooling around. Get me back into me proper skin. And . . . and find me a bite to eat. Whatever would Fiona say . . . if she knew ye'd clean forgotten me morning biscuits?"

Kevin's head felt as though it would burst wide open. How could this boy know about his Aunt Fiona, or that Kevin had forgotten to feed Tim? And if this wasn't really happening, *where* was Tim and *who* was this red-headed lunatic from out of the pond? Kevin took several deep breaths and stared into the distance. When he looked back, the boy was still there, now gazing trustfully up at him— just as Tim had done!

Kevin swallowed hard. "I don't believe this, and don't think I do, okay? Probably I'll wake up and find out it's only some wacko dream. . . ."

His voice trailed off as the boy in the grass toppled over while attempting to scratch himself with one foot.

"But," continued Kevin weakly, "we might as well play this thing for real until I do wake up. Okay. You want everything to be the way it was before. So, how could we do that?" He forced himself to consider the problem seriously. "Well, maybe the 'changeover' will sort of undo itself if we reverse the action. Why don't you—"

"—*Wash* it all away!" interrupted the boy, and promptly slid into the water.

Kevin watched as he ducked below the surface. A moment later the murky waters parted again. An auburn tuft emerged—but the long, wide-eyed face that followed was human still.

"Hey, Kevin!" Tim spluttered. "Nothing happened!"

"No kidding. You might have let me finish talking before you rushed off on your own, Tim! Like I was *trying* to say—why don't you do again exactly what you did the first time, only in reverse. Like running a filmstrip backward, see? Maybe then you'll 'unwind' the changeover."

Tim continued to look at him expectantly, so Kevin went on. "We know that the change happened when you were in the water. So duck under and then leap out onto the bank backward. Then run back up the slope to the exact place in the grass where you started out from. And last of all, lie down in the same position you were in when you were a dog." Kevin shrugged. "I know it sounds nuts, but let's try it!"

With the help of some tall weeds, Tim hauled himself into an upright position for the first time. He stepped confidently forward, wavered like an oversized toddler, and sat back down, hard. Blushing at Kevin's startled laughter, he cried hotly, "'Tis all plain foolishness, it is—rearin' upright on two hind legs when four will hold you steadier and carry you on faster, too!"

But he rose gamely to his feet again, and after several false starts managed to maintain his balance. Once he was steady on his feet, learning to run and even jump came more easily. Soon Tim was dashing about the meadow behind Kevin in a wild game of follow-the-leader.

When it came to unwinding the spell, they were not as successful. Despite Tim's repeating his former actions at the pond both forward and backward, on two feet and all fours, with his eyes open and shut, it was no use. He remained unremittingly human.

At last he sank to the ground, whimpering hopelessly.

"Cut that out, Tim!" cried Kevin, squatting beside him equally hot and frustrated. "Actually, you should be flattered to be human. I mean, humans are a higher species of animal than dogs."

"Och, Kevin, I'm not so sure about that," Tim growled. "So you humans can talk—big deal. We dogs do just fine without all them squawky noises. And if you're so much smarter, Kevin Mason, why am I still sittin' around in this sorry-looking pink skin?"

Kevin glared. "Well, being human sure hasn't improved you any," he retorted. "You're just as impatient as when you were a dog."

Tim thought that over and then sat up, rubbing his eyes. "Sorry, Kevin. It's just that everything has gone strange on me all at once. Here I am with me head wobblin' about so high off the ground it's like to fall and smash entirely and me poor eyes all raw from the sudden bright colors jabbin' in at them." He sighed. "But what use would Fiona have for a lad like I am now? She needs a fine purebred dog such as me former self, Kevin. Now who will be guidin' her about and showin' her off proud in those big dirt rings she loves so well?"

Suddenly Kevin's skin crawled. Tim was right! If Aunt Fiona's plans to establish a dog kennel were to succeed, she'd definitely need her prize Irish setter. But *he* was still as lost as when he'd first run off into the woods.

After a moment's silence, Kevin rose. "We've got to get help, Tim, but I don't know where," he said. "No one who didn't see it happen will believe about your changeover. Hey, I can't even believe it myself!"

Tim raised his tousled head. "Fiona would believe it. Why, she's always tellin' about the wee folk and magical charms."

"Well, Fiona's not here, and I hope she never finds out either," said Kevin emphatically. Then he started and looked at his watch. "Wow, it's almost eleven-thirty. Richie will think we're not coming. I hope he didn't go to my house looking for me!"

"Well, no one would be home, right?" said Tim.

"Yeah, that's good. But we've got to get to him right away. Look, Tim, if we meet anyone besides Richie, just be quiet and watch me for clues on what to do." Kevin gave Tim an appraising glance. "You'll look fine once we get some clothes on you. Here, wrap my shirt around your waist for now. I've got extra stuff at the tent."

As they crossed the meadow again, Tim tugged at Kevin's sleeve. "I've been thinkin', Kevin. I still want to be a dog again, but I'll miss havin' all the lovely words there ready at me tongue. It's like everything I ever heard spoken was packed away inside me head just waitin' to be used. Lucky that your Aunt Fiona filled me ears with chatter all day long."

Kevin nodded absently. They had reached the verge of the woods again, and he was looking about helplessly. "Darn it, Tim," he said. "I have no idea how to get back to our campsite from here."

"Truly, Kevin? Why, any dog worth his kibble could get you there and back without blinking an eye."

"Is that so? You weren't much help when we got lost before," Kevin accused him huffily.

"When *you* got lost before," corrected Tim. "Sure an' weren't you dragging me along by the neck all the while? I could scarcely draw breath, no less lead us in the right direction." And Tim managed to stalk off with an air of injured dignity in spite of his bare feet and flapping red loincloth.

"How could I trust you to do anything right after you ran off on me?" Kevin demanded, hurrying along behind him. "I was afraid you were going totally goofy again."

Tim turned around with a good-natured grin. "Well, p'raps I *was* after a bit o' fun with old Longears, Kevin."

With Tim leading the way, the walk back seemed amazingly short. Once they were inside the tent, Kevin retrieved his old cutoff jeans and a yellow T-shirt for Tim. "Now, let me take off that dog collar and you can try these on."

Tim allowed the leather band around his neck to be unbuckled and stowed in Kevin's backpack. Then began the struggle to get him into some clothes. It was like trying to dress a giant squid.

"Oh, to have me comfortable coat of fur back again," moaned Tim. Even with Kevin helping, he managed to thrust both feet into one leg of Kevin's cutoffs. "Hey, Kevin, this cloth stuff is made from a million little strings all tied together—and every single one of them is slicin' into me pitiful naked skin!"

Kevin had a hard job to keep from laughing. "It could be that my pants are a little small for you. Too bad I can't fasten that snapper at the waist."

"So, I'll leave it open then," said Tim. "And

how can we stop your shirt from sawin' me armpits in two, Kevin?"

"Sorry about that. Let's see, I guess you'll have to wear my thongs on your feet. Don't worry if your heels hang out the back." Privately, Kevin knew that he wouldn't be caught dead in that outfit.

As they entered Richie's yard and approached the house, Tim began to hang back. "I don't want to go in there with you. I'll just sorta nose around back here."

Kevin agreed readily. "Okay, I'll be right back with Rich and the food, Tim. Keep out of sight until I get here." To Kevin's astonishment the Owens' back door was locked and there was no sign of life inside the house. He ran around to the front of the house and rang the bell. From across the street a shrill voice hailed him. A few minutes later a gray-haired woman came puffing up the driveway toward him.

"You're Kevin Mason, aren't you, sonny?" she panted. "I'm Mrs. Panteese. I promised Richie Owen I'd keep an eye out for you. I'm to tell you that his grandma was taken bad with a stroke and his family had to hurry back to Cape Cod again."

"Oh no," said Kevin, sagging down onto the worn steps.

She took a wheezing breath and looked at him sympathetically. "I'm real sorry. Camping out, weren't you? My kids used to do that years ago, rain or frost. . . ."

Her friendly rambling was interrupted by a loud crash from behind the house. Just as Kevin and the old woman rounded the corner into the backyard, a sheepish Tim leaped to his feet beside an overturned garbage can. His uncombed red hair fell over his forehead like a fiery haystack. One hand was holding together the zipper of his too-small shorts and in the other, he grasped a scrap of pizza dripping with coffee grounds.

·:) **4** (:·

Garbage picking! That was disgraceful, even for a dog. Kevin was torn between pretending he didn't know the blushing figure beside the fallen trash can and hustling Tim away before Mrs. Panteese called the cops—or maybe the dogcatcher!

The old woman stared at Tim for a moment before finding her tongue. "Who are you, young man," she finally asked, "and just what are you doing there?"

"Wh-who, me?" Tim dropped the crust of

pizza as if it were red-hot. Stalling for time, he pulled the can upright with elaborate care and twisted it solidly into the ground before answering. "Uh-h, I'm Tim, missus. I was just sorta waitin' . . . and sniffin' about like. . . ." His husky voice trailed off and he rolled his eyes frantically at Kevin for help.

"Oh, Mrs. Panteese," blurted Kevin, "this is my friend Tim. He always gets clumsy and knocks things over . . . um, when he's upset. Yeah, and he's real upset today because . . . because his pants are too tight. I mean, those are actually mine. Y'see, Tim went swimming this morning and when he came out . . . um-m, he didn't have any clothes, so I loaned him my extra stuff. Then we came back here to get Richie. Rich was supposed to bring the food for our camp-out because I was bringing the tent and stuff."

Mrs. Panteese seemed to accept Kevin's garbled explanation. "You mean someone stole Timmy's clothes while you were swimming? I heard that there's a gang of roughnecks hanging around those woods lately." She frowned.

"And it looks like you're out of luck with Richie's food, too. Why, you poor kids must be starving! I bet I could manage to scrape together some hamburgers and a stack of french fries in no time. My kids always said that my burgers would make even Ronald McDonald turn green with envy."

Kevin shook his head regretfully, knowing that Tim wasn't ready for polite company yet. But his swift excuse, "Oh no, thanks, we really don't have time," went unheard as Tim rushed to the old woman's side.

"Real meat hamburgers, Mrs. Panties?" Tim cried, all shyness forgotten. "Och, what a wonderful idea! Sure an' there's an empty hole in me middle the size of a . . . a hay barn." And he herded her rapidly back down the driveway.

Kevin looked after them angrily. Tim hadn't listened to a word he'd said. "Stupid jerk!" he muttered. "So handle your own problems, then. I hope Mrs. Panteese sends you to the state funny farm!"

Immediately a horrid picture flashed into

his mind. It was of Tim tearing frantically along behind a wire fence, chased by a mob of white-coated attendants waving a straight-jacket. Kevin sighed and pelted down the driveway after the two retreating figures.

Inside Mrs. Panteese's comfortable old farmhouse, Kevin's apprehension grew. Just in time he prevented Tim from flopping onto a small rug beneath the kitchen table. Shoving him firmly into a chair, Kevin sat down beside him.

The fragrance of frying meat soon filled the room. Tim managed to slip away from Kevin and plant himself next to Mrs. Panteese at the stove. He gazed at her worshipfully. "Sure an' I can see by your gray hair that you're very old," he said, "but you can cook real good."

A wry smile crossed the woman's face. "Oh, I'm not too ancient to rustle up a good feed now and then," she replied. "I just hope you don't burst out of those tight little shorts before you're done eating it. By the way, Timmy, how come Kevin's clothes weren't stolen when yours were?"

Tim didn't once lift his eyes from the fry

pan. "Kevin didn't go swimmin', missus. But I was so hot, me tail was draggin', so I jumped in. That pond water was really magical, y'know. But when I climbed out and saw my bare . . ."

"Say, Mrs. Panteese," Kevin interrupted loudly, "can we pour ourselves a glass of water? I'm getting thirstier and thirstier just listening to Tim." Behind her back he gestured violently, pressing a finger across his lips.

But Tim only blundered off in a new direction. "I don't want *water*, Kevin. I'm tired of that. Let's have some of that ale stuff, or . . . or whiskey soda."

"Some *what*?" Mrs. Panteese whirled around, a shocked expression on her face. "I hope you're just being humorous, young man. In this house you'll have to settle for either water or milk. And one more thing. My name is Pan*teese*—rhymes with *geese*."

She raised her eyebrows at Kevin and went to the refrigerator for the milk. When Kevin joined her with two glasses, she whispered to him, "Your friend is a handsome boy, but isn't he a little strange?"

"Strange?" Kevin's hands trembled. "Er-r, not really. Tim just came over from Ireland, Mrs. Panteese, and sometimes he gets a little mixed up."

Mrs. Panteese had to hurry back to the frying meat, so she didn't see Tim hunch over his glass of milk and lap eagerly across the surface with his tongue. Exasperated, Kevin stretched a foot under the table and clipped him sharply in the shins. Tim yelped. The milk spilled.

"Why'd ye kick me like that, Kevin, just when I'm tryin' to drink out of this silly little glass? I'll never be able to understand you hum—" He stopped abruptly, aware of Mrs. Panteese's close attention and Kevin's warning glare. "Oh. That is . . . I'll never understand you hum-*erous Americans*," he finished triumphantly.

Kevin felt the knot of anger and resentment that had been growing inside him begin to melt. Tim had covered his flub just fine this time. How could they ever have explained away Tim's use of the words "*you* humans"? He gave his friend a conspiratorial wink.

From that point on the meal proceeded smoothly. Tim watched Kevin eat his hamburger and managed to refrain from bolting his own in one mouthful. He chewed noisily but with such blissful enjoyment that Mrs. Panteese's attitude warmed noticeably. She cooked up seconds of everything and then sat down with them to drink a cup of coffee.

"You two boys don't have to pack up that tent and go home just because Richie isn't here," she assured them. "Since his parents have already okayed the camp-out in their field, I'm sure it will be okay to stay. Just don't light any fires. I'll be right here across the road in case you have an emergency."

Kevin heaved a sigh of relief. "Oh, that's great, Mrs. Panteese. I was beginning to think I'd *never* get to use my new camping stuff. We won't be any bother to you, I promise."

The old woman nodded. "I know that being away on your own is half the fun of a camp-out, so I'll just donate some bread and milk for later on tonight. You two might as well help yourself to whatever you want at the Owens' farm stand. It will only go bad if it stays there until they get back."

"I have some money," said Kevin. He knew that Mrs. Owen kept an honor system cashbox on the counter for customers who came when she wasn't there. "Tomorrow we'll go back to my house for more supplies."

Mrs. Panteese ran an amused eye over Timothy's bulging stomach and gaping clothes. "I don't know if *you'll* make it that far, Timmy. Looks to me like the seams in those shorts are headed for a major split. Here, let me dig around in the old-clothes chest and see if I can't come up with something left over from one of my boys."

As they finished their milk, they could hear her rummaging around in some boxes in a back bedroom. A few minutes later she emerged, holding aloft a pair of faded overalls. "These should fit those long legs of yours, Timmy. How old are you now, young man?"

Tim had been lolling back in his chair, his eyes glazed with well-fed contentment. "Och, I really don't know for sure," he drawled lazily.

Kevin gasped, and choked painfully on a swallow of milk. Fortunately his sputtering distracted Mrs. Panteese's attention from Tim's careless reply. When he regained his breath, he shoved Tim and the faded denims toward an adjoining bathroom. "Go try these on. And get your brains together!" he hissed through gritted teeth.

By the time Tim emerged, he was not only dressed in blue overalls, but he was also alert again. "Thanks fer these, Mrs. Panties," he said gravely. "And as I was tellin' ye before about me age—I'm sorta in-between at the moment. Isn't that about right, Kevin?"

With a pang, Kevin realized that that was the best answer Tim was able to come up with. He really didn't know how old he was.

"That's right," he replied. "Tim and I are both about the same age—elevenish going on twelve."

He rose and carried his dishes carefully to the sink, hoping that Tim would do so, too. It was time to leave. He didn't think he could cope with any more awkward questions.

Tim cooperated. "We'll be thankin' ye fer the lovely meal, Mrs. Panties. It was the best I've ever eaten me whole life long," he said, once again bringing a smile to her lips.

"You are very welcome, boys. I'd almost forgotten how . . . interesting young people can be." She packed up some bread and a jar of milk and accompanied them to the door.

After crossing the road to Richie's house, they stopped by the small farm stand at the driveway. "Let's get some of these pears for breakfast," suggested Kevin. "We can have lettuce and tomato sandwiches tonight."

Tim shrugged. His stomach was still full, and he wasn't much interested in fruits or vegetables.

The heat of the sun was already fading by the time they returned to the tent.

"What a break that Mrs. Panteese said it was okay for us to stay here," Kevin said as they put away the food. "There's no way I could have gone back home tonight with you in tow instead of Fiona's dog. Mom would never have believed what happened. She'd have zapped me over to the nearest psychiatrist to see if my brain had gone dead."

"Well, ye'd better get me out of this mess soon, Kevin, or I'll need that psy-cat-rist thing meself." Tim placed a hand on Kevin's arm. "Why were ye flashin' yer fangs at me so when I told Mrs. Panties that she cooks good even though she's old?"

Kevin thought a moment. "It just sounded kind of rude, Tim. As if you were hoping she wouldn't be carted off to a nursing home before she could finish frying up the meat, y'know?"

Tim snorted in exasperation. "What *should* I have said then?" he demanded. "You mean, like—'Och, Mrs. Panties, 'tis surely a magical feast you're makin' us, bein' that you're as young and dainty as the fairy queen herself'!"

Kevin doubled over with laughter, just imagining Mrs. Panteese's astonishment. He tried again to explain himself. "I guess I'm just talking about being polite. You know, trying not to hurt people's feelings. Get it? Hey, pal, do you want them to think you're an insensitive ignoramus?"

Tim was impressed by the big words, as Kevin knew he would be. He rolled them around on his tongue. "In-sensi-tive ig-nor-a-mus. Sure an' it has a grand and satisfyin' sound to it, Kevin Mason." He shook his tousled red head emphatically. "An insensitive ignoramus I shall ever try to be."

Kevin turned his head away to hide his smile. Tim obviously hadn't grasped the meaning of the words, but it was too good a joke to spoil yet. He grabbed up the Frisbee. "C'mon, Tim, it's time for you to learn to play this game like a human."

"Sure thing, Kevin," returned Tim, bounding after him. "Just as soon as you learn to catch that thing in your mouth like a dog!"

⋅⋅ᢓ 5 ᢗ⋅⋅

The next morning dawned clear but a bit chilly. Kevin was awakened by Tim tossing about on the air mattress and grumbling about not having his nice warm coat of fur. Without opening his eyes, Kevin groaned softly. "Are you still talking, Tim? I was hoping that I'd wake up this morning and find that your changeover into a human body had been just a bad dream."

"A dream? You mean like pictures in your head while you're sleeping?" Tim asked, sitting up. "I didn't know that humans had them, too."

Kevin crawled out of his sleeping bag. "Let's get going, Tim. We've got to find a way to turn you back into a dog again. In the meantime, we'll have to get some more food and stuff at my house."

A short while later they were walking quickly along the winding trail that led through sparsely wooded fields to town. Kevin was making a mental list of the supplies they'd need to pick up at home. Tim ranged energetically from one side to the other, stopping to poke into rodent holes or chase the squirrels that crisscrossed their path. Finally he tired of this and ran up alongside Kevin.

"I like this shortcut," he said. "It's more fun than walking along that hot road with cars spraying rocks at you. Why didn't we come this way yesterday?"

Kevin turned to his companion. Already the long, thin face had become as familiar to him as that of an old friend. "I only use this trail when I'm in a hurry," he said. "It leads past a broken-down shack by the railroad where some high school guys like to hang out and give the younger kids a hard time. Probably they have summer jobs by now and we won't even see them."

A look of surprise crossed Tim's face. "You're afraid of those guys, aren't you? They must be like the hooligans who torment penned-in dogs at home. Fiona says that if you just stay cool and don't let them get you excited, they'll soon get bored and leave you alone."

"Oh sure!" Kevin replied. "I can't imagine why Richie and I didn't think of that when those two big apes were chasing us through the woods!"

He could feel his muscles tense as they rounded a bend and entered a dark underpass where the train tracks passed above them. He hated it in there. It was creepy and damp, with massive timbers overhead that dripped dirty water into his hair. It was the perfect place for an ambush.

Much to his relief they emerged safely into

the brilliant sunshine on the other side. They stood still a moment, looking about. No one was in sight, and the dilapidated little shack squatting close to the embankment appeared to be abandoned.

"Let's take a look inside, Kevin. Maybe we can find out what they do here," said Tim, bounding forward.

Kevin followed him, still feeling uneasy. "Why bother? It's just some kind of a stupid clubhouse."

The battered green door didn't budge, so Tim circled to the back of the cabin. "Hey, come around here, Kevin. There's a window," called Tim in a low voice.

Side by side they rubbed clear spaces in the grimy glass and, cupping their hands around their eyes, tried to peer into the interior.

All was a bluish haze. Then, to Kevin's horror, several pale blobs inside took shape and seemed to move toward them. Without a word he pulled Tim's arm and they turned to run.

At one corner of the shack, a glowering

teenager with long greasy hair appeared, blocking their path. A second, cigarette dangling from the corner of his mouth, moved in from the other direction.

The smoker stared at Kevin for a second and then grabbed both boys roughly by the arm. "Get moving," he commanded in a gravelly voice.

"So what are you going to do—shoot us for looking in your window?" Kevin asked boldly. But he and Tim both hastened to obey.

As they approached the front of the cabin, their captor called out, "Hey, Sam, you won't believe who's sneaking around here again!"

Sam, short but muscular, was leaning against a tree with his arms crossed. His eyes glittered behind half-opened lids. "*You*," he said to Kevin, "get your butt over here."

Kevin took a hesitant step forward, aware of Tim crowding in behind him.

"It's the little punk we chased away a couple of weeks ago!" said Sam. "You and your buddies stupid or somethin'? Now read my lips, kid—GET OUT AND STAY OUT!"

At this, Tim pushed forward, giving a 'leave-this-to-me' nod. "Hi, my name is Tim," he said politely. "Kevin and I were just passing by, and we thought that your place here looked kind of interesting. I bet you're one of those"—he rolled back his eyes, searching for the most impressive phrase he knew—"insensitive ignoramuses Kevin was telling me about. We—" He was interrupted by a howl of rage as Sam charged him. Instinctively Tim dodged sideways, and it was Kevin who was pinned against the shack in a bone-crunching hold.

"Ow! Let go of me!" Kevin yelled. "He didn't mean what he said—he's not from around here."

Another teenager, in a frayed denim vest, ran out of the shack, trailing a ragged cloud of acrid smoke. "Hang on to 'im!" he shouted. "I'm sick of those twerps spying on us all the time."

Tim, now several paces to Kevin's left, swung around to face the newcomer. Kevin could see the hair at the base of Tim's neck rise stiffly. A menacing rumble sounded in his throat.

"Hey, what's with that Looney Tunes redhead? Go get him, guys," shouted Sam. "Let's teach them a *real* lesson this time!"

The newcomer in the vest lunged after Tim, who darted swiftly through the trees. His pursuer soon gave up and returned to his friends. "Forget the redhead. He's already too scared to spit," he boasted. "And this one will be, too, when I'm finished with him."

Kevin was truly frightened now. These guys were showing off for one another, each sounding tougher than the last. He twisted frantically in his captor's hold. "Look, we didn't see a thing. We were just passing through on the way home, so let me go and there won't be any trouble."

The older boys pressed closer. Their faces were hard.

"Is the little punk making threats, or what?" sneered Sam. He released Kevin into the center of the tight circle. "He says that if we let him go, he won't make no trouble for us. Hey, let's show him how worried we are!"

The long-haired boy hooted scornfully and swung both arms stiff against Kevin's chest, shoving him backward against Sam. Sam spun Kevin around and knocked him toward the wearer of the denim vest, who threw him to his neighbor. And so it went, on around the circle, faster and faster.

Dizzy and aching, Kevin struggled to stay upright until one knee buckled and he slammed down onto his back.

The bullies closed in over him.

Suddenly a roar of outrage split the air. Snarling and wolf-wild, Tim hurtled into the midst of the tight circle. The unexpected collision of bodies sent one teenager spinning aside and another sprawling against him. Still raging, Tim leaped onto Sam with bared teeth and ripped his T-shirt down the back.

"Help! Get this maniac off me!" shrieked Sam. "He bit me, man. He *bit* me!"

Recovering his wits, Kevin sprang to his feet. He rammed his head into the middle of the denim vest bearing down on him. There was a satisfying grunt and the teenager staggered backward, doubled up in pain.

"C'mon, Tim!" Kevin shouted, and took off like a jackrabbit. When he didn't hear Tim's footsteps pounding along behind him, he turned to look.

The terrorized Sam had fallen under Tim's weight and lay on his side, cringing. Tim was crouched above him with his teeth only inches from the youth's thick neck.

The others were just beginning to stir from the initial shock of attack.

Kevin could feel hysteria rising in his throat. "Get out of there *now*, Tim!" he cried, and then commandingly, "Timothy, come!"

Tim looked up as if rousing from a trance. He rose reluctantly and then ran off after Kevin. Not until the first houses of the town could be seen through the trees did Kevin dare to slow their pace.

"Whoa, Tim, hold it a second," he gasped. "I have a terrible stitch in my side." He dropped to the ground under a tree, clutching his ribs. After he caught his breath, he looked over at his companion. "Wow, that was a close escape, wasn't it?"

Tim sat down beside Kevin, panting with his tongue out. "Sure an' that bunch was meaner than old Muggins with a beef bone. They were knockin' you around just for the fun of it!"

"Yeah. I was really scared. Thanks for coming to my rescue, Tim. You crashed right into the middle of them, howling like a blood-thirsty timber wolf!"

Tim sat up and a huge grin spread across his face. "*Did* I then, Kevin? I can't rightly remember what happened after they grabbed you. And if ye hadn't lectured me about bein' so polite, I'd have gladly sunk me teeth into that Sam guy—instead o' giving his T-shirt the tiniest bit of a nibble."

Kevin laughed until the stitch in his side stabbed like a hot dagger. "Oh-ho, Tim, that was some polite little nibble," he said when he could talk again. "Somehow I don't think the guy even appreciated your good manners."

He sat quietly for a moment and then added, "You didn't think once about the odds, did you, Tim—four high school guys against us two. You just charged in with everything you had."

Tim cocked his head to one side and regarded Kevin seriously. "Sure an' what else would I do? 'Twould be a poor sort of a dog to worry about his own skin when a human he loves needs help!"

Kevin's eyes misted at Tim's simple answer. "Well, I don't know if I'd have had the guts," he said. "You know what, Tim? Maybe we should give up trying to change you back. How about we two just take off for California together?"

"What do you mean? What is this Cali-forya thing?" asked Tim warily.

"It's a great place about three thousand miles west of here. The sun always shines there, and the people are sorta laid back and no one cares about how anyone acts or looks. You could blend right into that scene!"

"But, Kevin," protested Tim, "Fiona would never be able to find me so far away! We can't give up already. You promised me that . . ."

"Okay, okay!" Kevin interrupted him.

"Let's just keep it as a backup plan, then. But we'd have a lot of fun together, Tim. You're the best friend I have."

"*And* the most insensitive ignoramus, right?" asked Tim.

Kevin's serious mood evaporated. With a cackle of laughter, he got to his feet. "Maybe I'd better explain about that on the way back to my house."

6

"*Hey, Tim, come on! We don't have time to fool* around looking at stuff," Kevin yelled back over his shoulder. Ever since they'd reached Main Street, Tim had begun to lag farther and farther behind.

At the moment, Tim was standing on a sun-baked street corner, sniffing the air eagerly. "Hold up a minute," he called. "I've just had a grand idea."

Kevin frowned and went back. He was still shaken by their encounter in the woods. Now he was anxious to get their supplies from home and get back to the solitary safety of the tent, where he could figure out their next move.

"It's about this, uh, trans . . . transformation thing, Kevin," Tim began as his friend approached. "You were sayin' before that no adults would be able to believe that I'm really a dog, right?"

"Right!" Again Kevin checked his companion over from head to toe. Tim looked like a perfectly normal boy—healthy and even handsome in a lanky sort of way. He shook his head. "If *I* can hardly believe it, there's no way anyone else will."

"But why are you so sure?" persisted Tim. "You never even tried telling anyone. Don't you think Mrs. Panties might have suspected somethin'? And those guys in the woods— they looked at me real queer-like."

"They did? No *kidding*! And there you were, acting like any ordinary, everyday kind of a guy," teased Kevin. "Oh, they suspected something, all right. It was that you're totally nuts. Uh-uh, Tim, we've got to get you back to your old self on our own. Let's go."

Tim didn't move. "But what about an animal doctor? Surely he'd help us once he examined me and found out the truth." His voice rose eagerly. "Kevin, there's a vet's office somewhere close by here. The odor of medicine and scared animals is fairly burnin' me nostrils. Please, can't we just try it?"

Kevin shrugged his shoulders and then followed Tim around the corner. A veterinarian probably *was* the best bet they had, so why was he feeling so reluctant? And then he knew. He was in no hurry to lose the companionship of this human Tim—this spirited friend and faithful ally. But he also knew that Tim's deepest wish was to be a dog again.

Just as Tim had predicted, there was a veterinary office close by. On a post outside a gray-shingled house, they saw a neat rectangular sign that read DAVID A. MASSEY, D.V.M.

As they went up the front walk and mounted the steps, Kevin racked his brain for a reasonable way to explain to the vet what they wanted. He drew a complete blank.

A blond receptionist looked up from her desk in the waiting room as they entered. Eyeing the two boys narrowly, she asked, "Where's your pet?"

Right away, Kevin knew this was going to be bad. "Uh-h. Oh, my . . . *pet?*" he repeated as if he'd never heard the word before. She continued to stare, so he pointed quickly to Tim and stammered, "H-he's it. I mean, it's him."

"That boy is your pet? Now see here, young man, this is a doctor's office just like any other, and we can't waste time . . ."

She was interrupted by a deep chuckle from the room behind her desk and a man's voice called out through the open door, "Send those jokers in, Audrey. I have a few minutes before I scrub for surgery. I'll deal with them."

Kevin hadn't felt so much like a fool in years. He jabbed Tim in the side as they walked into the well-lighted office. "This was your idea, pal," he whispered. "Handle it yourself!"

A pleasant young man with a trimmed brown beard lounged against a chrome examination table. "Okay, I'll presume that neither of you young men would claim to be a pet pussycat," he said, smiling, "so one of you must be a dog, right?"

"Och, doctor, I just knew ye'd understand!" cried Tim, his face shining with relief. "We're in desperate need of help. 'Twas only yesterday, see, when I got switched into me present form. Kevin and I were in the fields and suddenly this brazen old hare leaps out and flirts its tail right under me nose. Now, bein' that I'm an Irish setter—a bird dog, y'know—I'm not supposed to chase those silly creatures atal', but this one was practically between me teeth from the start. Only—"

As Tim rattled on, the doctor's bearded face was wreathed in a broad grin. And when he described climbing out of the pond only to find himself two-legged and naked, without a tuft of his shiny coat or an inch of his beautiful plumed tail, the young vet threw back his head and laughed aloud. He came around his long table and clapped Tim on the back.

"What a story—and from an Irish setter, of course! Well, my boy, *you'll* never need to kiss the Blarney stone. Your gift of the gab already outdoes that of any Irishman I've heard yet."

Tim's face fell. "Blarney? But—but you said you knew that I'm a dog! Oh, doctor, if you're not believin' me, give me a rabies test or somethin'. Oh, please get me out of this bloody human body!"

Still smiling, the young man glanced at his watch. His manner became brisk. "Sorry, boys. I don't know what you're up to, but I've run out of time. Here, hustle out this side door. Good luck with your little game, whatever it is." They could hear him chuckling as the door closed behind them.

Tim's face was red with frustration. Kevin turned to him and said, "I *told* you he wouldn't believe one word you said."

"Well, you were partly wrong, too!" cried Tim. "He didn't think I was crazy, but just havin' a bit o' fun with him."

"Oh yeah? Toward the end there he was

beginning to wonder. I could see it in his eyes," Kevin retorted.

He stalked down the street, followed at a distance by Tim, who maintained an aloof silence all the way to Kevin's house.

Once inside the Masons' kitchen, they forgot their tiff in the rush to gather up supplies. Kevin ran upstairs to borrow a pair of his father's thongs for Tim. When he returned, he found Tim deep in the pantry closet, pulling down boxes.

"Aha! So this is what ye keep up on the shelves," said Tim, looking about greedily. "All sorts of lovely goodies, squeezed into little jars and boxes. I was hopin', Kevin, that you'd not mind if I took a wee taste here and there."

"Now cut it out, Tim, we don't have time for tasting. I told you we're just going to pick up enough to tide us over. Sandwich stuff, apples, soda, and that's it."

"Aw-w, Kevin. But surely it'll be no trouble to take along just this one darlin' little brown cake." He held up a box of chocolate cake mix with a mouth-watering picture on the outside.

"No, we can't. That's just a powder now. It has to be mixed and baked before you can eat it," Kevin said impatiently.

But Tim's nose was pressed against the box lid and he inhaled the aroma blissfully. "'Sall right," he murmured, "I'll lick it straight out of the wrapper."

Then his eyes flew open again. "Hist! I hear a motor, Kevin. Someone's coming to the house!"

Kevin sprang to the window and held the curtain aside. "It's my mother! We either have to hide or try to explain—and we know that won't work. Quick, back inside!"

He shoved Tim into the pantry, grabbed their supplies off the table, and piled in, closing the door behind him.

Only seconds later a key rattled in the lock and a pair of high-heeled shoes clicked across the linoleum kitchen floor. Kevin recognized the clink of kettle against faucet as it was filled and placed on the stove. Then the footsteps paused.

"Kevin?" his mother's voice called. "Are you

home, Kevin?"

Kevin held his breath. Had she seen something or simply half sensed their presence? Oh, he should never have hidden in this stupid trap of a closet like some kind of a sneak. Now he'd have to explain that, as well as all the rest.

The footsteps drew nearer. Passing by, they proceeded to the foot of the stairs. "Are you up there, Kev?" Mrs. Mason called uncertainly. After waiting a moment, she sighed and returned to the kitchen.

Inside the closet, Tim grinned at Kevin and softly opened the door a crack. He seemed to be enjoying himself, but Kevin was embarrassed. He felt like an outsider spying into the private moments of his mother's life. She even looked different to him now—tired and thin-faced.

Several minutes passed as Mrs. Mason put a load of clothes into the dryer and another into the washer, made herself lunch, and sat down to eat. Through the crack the boys saw her turn and push the playback button on the telephone message machine.

The first caller on the tape was a co-worker at the real estate office, and then, after a series of clicks, Fiona's clear voice filled the kitchen. Kevin placed a hand firmly over Tim's quivering arm and listened intently.

Fiona's message was brief. She would be finished with her business arrangements early the next day and planned to arrive back at Logan Airport at one o'clock.

Mrs. Mason groaned, "Oh no, I'll never make it in time."

Picking up the phone, she dialed a long number and asked to speak to Mr. John Mason with the Tanner Ballbearing Company.

"Hello, John," she said at last. "Sorry to call you off the convention floor, but I need a favor. Can you pick up Fiona about one o'clock tomorrow? I'll be tied up at a house closing, so I can't go."

After a brief silence she replied, "No, I understand. I'll just order one of those airport limos to meet her. What? . . . No, I haven't heard from Kevin, but it's early yet."

Another silence. "No, he'll be careful, John. He knows how much Tim means to Fiona." She listened again and then said, "Maybe it was *all* a mistake. We thought Kevin would love living here—a real house, smaller school, and the freedom to roam the countryside. But until now he just hung around and found reasons to avoid helping out." Her voice softened. "Oh, I know he's a good kid and I guess it will work out. Well, I've got to run now. Bye John."

Kevin's ears felt suddenly numb. She'd been talking about *him*! He scarcely noticed his mother dial a limousine service, straighten up the kitchen, and leave.

As soon as the sound of the retreating motor faded, Tim burst from the closet. "Did you hear my Fiona's voice in that little box, Kevin? She says she's coming back tomorrow afternoon!"

"Yeah, I know," he said quietly. Tim, he realized, had only focused on the part of the conversation that concerned himself. But maybe he wasn't the only one with a single-track mind.

Abruptly, Kevin pulled over the telephone notepad. He scribbled a few lines to his mother telling her that they'd been home and were both fine. Then, lost in his own thoughts, Kevin waited for Tim to finish packing the food.

It wasn't until they were well on their way that Kevin noticed the weight of the overloaded grocery bag he was carrying. Glaring at Tim's similar burden, he yelled, "Hey, we were only getting sandwich stuff and something to drink, remember? So how come we have *two* big bags?"

7

Tim smiled sheepishly and hugged his bulging grocery bag against his chest. "Och, Kevin, there were so many tempting smells in your pantry that I couldn't choose between them. So I just took a bit o' this and that. How was I to know that we'd have to lug them the long way back to the tent?"

"Oh, maybe you'd rather use the path again and have another go at the tough guys?" Kevin could see by Tim's rapt attention that he was taking the idea seriously. He shook his head emphatically. "No way, Tim. We play it safe this time."

"Well, then, I have a grand idea how we can lighten our loads," said Tim eagerly.

"What's that—drop the bananas in the book slot at the library?" Kevin nodded toward the white wooden building with four tall pillars that was on the other side of the street.

Tim threw back his head and bayed joyfully. "Och, Kevin, 'tis a joker you are, fer sure. But no, I was meanin' that it must be time fer lunch by now. The more we chow down now, the less we have left to carry, right?"

There was a certain logic here that appealed to Kevin, especially since he was starving, too. At an empty lot on the corner, the boys found seats on some overturned paint cans, and Tim began immediately to rummage in the food bags. He lined up his selections on the ground in front of him—sweet gherkin pickles, Twinkies, coconut breakfast bars, salted peanuts, and a large bag of potato chips, all to be washed down with warm ginger ale.

"Hey, Tim, you sure you want all that stuff at one meal?"

Tim was sure. He could hardly swallow one mouthful fast enough to make room for the next. After several hearty helpings, some of which still bulged inside his cheeks, he stopped abruptly in midchew. Clutching at his middle with both hands, he cried fearfully, "Kevin, somethin' terrible is happenin' inside here. Me stomach is on fire and I think me guts are about to explode entirely!" He moaned. "I'm *dyin*'. Tell Fiona how sorry I am."

Calmly, Kevin watched him roll sideways off his seat and curl up under a bush. "You'll live," he said. "It's only a stomachache from gobbling so fast. What's left in these grocery sacks?" He pulled them both over and dug about inside. "Oh, great—herbed stuffing, bread, chocolate cake mix, beef bouillon cubes . . . Hey, Tim, did you ever think that my mother might need some of this stuff?"

But Tim didn't answer. Kevin could see that he was too miserable to move. "Look, I have to take some of this back home. Also, I think

I should telephone Mom. She won't see my note until after work, and she'll be worried. You wait for me right here and take it easy until your stomach feels better. I'll see you in about ten minutes, okay?"

Tim's only reply was a groan that managed to convey that he didn't care whether he ever saw Kevin again.

Kevin packed up some of the unnecessary food in one bag and hurried off in the direction they'd come. A sudden heady sense of freedom put a bounce in his step. It was so great not having to watch out for Tim for a while.

When he let himself in the side door of his house a few minutes later, the gong on the hall clock was sounding. He listened in dismay. It was already twelve-thirty and he still hadn't an idea in his head about how to change Tim back. They needed more time! Could he possibly persuade his mother to let them camp out another night? Setting his jaw for some high-pressure salesmanship, he approached the telephone.

It turned out to be easier than Kevin had dared to hope. His mother was busy with a client but was relieved to hear from him. She seemed to think that since he and Tim had managed to survive a night in the tent already, the odds were with them. After a few standard questions, she agreed to let them stay one more night.

After he hung up the phone, Kevin re-shelved the food he'd brought back. On the way out again, he caught sight of his two overdue library books on the kitchen counter. The library! Now they'd have the time to get some books and read up on changeovers, metamorphoses, and transformations. Maybe there were some other cases like Tim's on record!

But the library had already closed for the day by the time Kevin got there. He slid his books through the drop located beside the front door and crossed to the empty lot where he'd left Tim. The remaining brown paper bag of food was right where he'd left it—but Tim was nowhere in sight.

A sense of foreboding crept over Kevin. He called. He shouted. He paced the lot, pushing aside clumps of ragweed and goldenrod, peering under slanting stacks of discarded roofing. No Tim.

Could someone have taken him away to the hospital? Even in his panic, Kevin rejected that notion. Stomachaches are pretty easy to figure out when the sick person is surrounded by empty junk food wrappers. No, Tim must have started to feel better and become bored with waiting for his friend to return.

In a fury of frustration, Kevin stalked into the street, bellowing Tim's name. Again there was no answer. Where could he be? The library was closed and the three identical houses on the next block were sealed up tight with their air conditioners humming. Aside from an abandoned construction site with high board fences all around it, the only other building close by was a grocery store on the corner. Yeah, maybe he'd wandered inside to cool off or something.

Even that hope faded as soon as Kevin

pushed through the glass door and found that he was the only customer in the little store. He backed out hurriedly and stood on the sidewalk, feeling helpless. Beads of cold sweat broke out on his forehead.

Don't panic now, don't panic, he warned himself. Maybe Tim went back to the campsite. Maybe he's there now, waiting for me. But when he passed the empty lot, the sight of the grocery bag sitting next to the bush made Kevin's heart sink again. He knew that Tim would not have gone back to the tent and left the food supplies behind. But then where . . . ?

Suddenly a dreadful vision filled his head. It was of the high board fence surrounding the building site near their lunch spot, and the warning signs plastered on it—KEEP OUT! DANGER! And Kevin knew with a stone-cold certainty that Tim was there at that very moment.

If only he had X-ray vision! As Kevin raced toward the high fence, his eyes searched for any boy-size hole through which Tim could have crawled. There were several. Falling to his knees beside the fence, Kevin squeezed through the nearest one. What he saw then stopped the breath in his throat.

The huge cellar excavation of the unfinished building yawned before him. Above it metal girders cast thin shadows across the few scattered floor beams that spanned its breadth. In the middle of one of them wavered Tim, his arms flailing as he fought for balance. As Kevin approached, one of Tim's muddy feet slipped off the board. He lurched forward and grasped the beam frantically with both hands, his body bent like a runner waiting for the starting gun—but with one foot still dangling in space.

The calm of desperation descended on Kevin. He moved swiftly to a position at the end of the beam. In a quiet voice he said, "Hi, Tim, you're going to be okay now. You've got a good two-handed hold on that beam. Hang on tight until your right foot is back aboard. Then you can stand and walk across to me."

Tim didn't seem surprised to find Kevin present. He answered in a strangled voice, without lifting his head, "Help me, Kevin! Me hands have turned to stone and I don't know where me one foot has gone to. I can't stand up—surely I'll fall and crack me skull open down below."

For a moment, Kevin considered going onto the beam himself to steady Tim, but he wasn't much of an acrobat and it looked too rickety to support more weight. Forcing himself to sound reassuring, he said, "Okay, no problem, Tim. Then just lower yourself and *sit* on the beam. You'll feel safer straddling it with a leg on each side. Then you can sort of hitch yourself toward me with your arms."

Quaking visibly, Tim managed to follow Kevin's directions. When he finally was able to lift his eyes to Kevin, they were wide with strain. "Whew! 'Tis better this way for sure, Kevin. But I'd give me last steak bone just to have four paws safely on the ground again."

Despite this lament, Tim began hunching himself slowly forward along the beam.

Finally he reached the end near Kevin, who helped him over to the dirt embankment.

Now that Tim was safe, Kevin's calm dissolved in a wave of fury. "You stupid idiot!" he yelled. "You . . . you putrid dog-breath jerk! How dare you go wandering around looking for trouble? Don't you know that I'm responsible for you and if anything bad happens, I'll never live it down?"

The ordeal behind him, Timothy allowed himself to become hurt. "You didn't have to call me that, Kevin. Is 'putrid dog-breath' your way of soundin' kind and polite?" He sniffed. "Anyway, I didn't just wander off. I started to feel better and you didn't come back. Then a yellow cat hissed at me and streaked off right straight through a space in that big fence. Hey, Kevin, you should have seen us tearin' across that old board—it was easy to do while I was chasin' the cat."

"So you were in there all along. Didn't you hear me calling you?"

Tim flushed. "Well, I might have heard something . . . but you sounded so angry that

I decided to wait. After the cat ran off, I did start back over the board again. Och, Kevin, I've never been so scared in me life! But then you came and made everything work out okay."

Kevin shuddered. "You could've been killed! Didn't you see all those red danger signs posted on the fence? What did you think they were—valentines?"

"Signs?" repeated Tim. "Oh, you mean those bloody-lookin' papers with the black marks . . . the writing, on them? You didn't tell me they meant danger."

An alarming suspicion dawned in Kevin's mind. "You don't know how to read and write, do you, Tim?"

Tim pulled back and gave Kevin an injured look. "And how should I know about those silly little hen scratch marks, Kevin?"

"What a jerk I am!" said Kevin grimly. "You're such a fast talker that I expected you to know all about language."

Looking down modestly, Tim said, "'Tis true that every word I've ever heard spoken seems stored in me brain—and makin' better sense to me each day. But all those scritchy black marks are a puzzlement entirely."

"Yeah, they would be. People need to be *taught* how to read and write. It takes years in school before you get good at it."

They crawled through the fence again and as they made their way back along the street, Kevin's face was serious. He had forgotten that in many ways the human world was an alien one to Tim. It hadn't been fair to leave Tim alone and then blame him for making mistakes.

Suddenly aware that his friend had spoken to him, Kevin discovered that Tim had found the food bag.

"I have a grand idea, Kevin," he said with mock innocence. "It's about suppertime now, so why don't we stop here and . . ."

He got no further, because Kevin snatched up a loaf of Italian bread and swatted him over the head with it.

·ᴐ 8 ɕ··

A ruddy sunset glowed above the maple trees as Tim settled himself against the large rock that was serving the boys as a backrest. He looked across at Kevin, sniffed the air questioningly, and then broke the silence. "You've hardly said a word since we got back to the tent, Kevin," he said. "What're you thinkin' about now?"

"Oh." Kevin snapped back to the present. "I have a lot to think about. For one thing I'm still quaking in my boots about the little tightrope act you did at that excavation. Also,

I'm trying to figure some new way to transform you back. And . . . well, I keep remembering what my mom and dad were saying over the phone at home."

"Yeah, really!" returned Tim. "We have to keep better track of the time tomorrow. When Fiona arrives home from the airport, I'd like to be right there, waggin' me tail."

"I'm talking about how my parents thought this move would be so good for *me*!" Kevin continued. "In fact, I've been kind of mad at them for dragging me here. I thought it was just so they could get a nice house and a new car and have big careers and all. Like they didn't much care how I felt about things. But now—well, I feel kind of good and kind of bad at the same time."

Tim's head tilted attentively and then he said, "Why should you feel bad, Kevin? I can't believe how someone at your house is always shouting at you to do this or why didn't you do that. My Fiona only shouts when the bad letters come from the bank."

Kevin felt like punching Tim. "Oh yeah?" he cried. "Don't forget that both my parents are working long hours now and they really need . . . help."

"Hey, why raise your ruff at me? I'm on your side," said Tim in an injured tone. "Hey, when your mom tells you to clean your bedroom, you practically roll the whole thing into a ball and stuff it out of sight. And I love those great-smelling socks under your bed!" Then a new thought struck him. "But how come you hang around the house so much, like your mom said on the phone, Kevin?"

"Why don't you just drop dead!" muttered Kevin. He looked closely at his companion's face but saw only genuine interest there. "Well, okay. To tell the truth, Tim, I'm not so great at making new friends," he admitted. "Back in the city there was always a bunch of kids at the park. You could play basketball or roller hockey, or just hang out. But here there's nothing, and it seemed that my parents were loading on the chores just to keep me busy while they're out."

"Oh," said Tim doubtfully. He yawned hugely, and his long tongue stretched out and curled like a paper birthday blower.

"Relax, Kevin, things will work out eventually, right?"

"Wrong!" Kevin cried. "It's not that simple! Things don't just 'work out,' Tim. Someone has to *do* something."

"I'm lucky, but most dogs learn that they just have to accept whatever comes their way," said Tim glumly.

"Well, I'm not a dog. And you'd better hope that I *don't* lay back and accept everything—or you'll be kissing your famous 'plume of a tail' good-bye forever!" Kevin rose, feeling tired but resolute. "Let's go to bed. I'm beat."

"Me, too. This has been a long, long day." Tim yawned again.

But once Kevin was inside his sleeping bag with Tim on the air mattress beside him, he found that he was too wound up to sleep. So much had happened in two days. It seemed impossible that he'd so recently left home to go camping with his aunt's dog . . . with Fiona's *dog*! . . . *Tim was a dog!*

Abruptly, Kevin sat up and grabbed his flashlight. Snapping it on, he pointed the circle of light at the air mattress beside him.

There lay the redheaded Tim. His lanky form was unmistakably human, and yet as Kevin watched, those long legs jerked spasmodically in a dream-run and the lips drew back in a toothy snarl.

Goose bumps prickled up and down Kevin's spine. Tim was only human on the outside. He'd been transformed from a bright dog to a bright boy, but his behavior and instincts were still all canine. Even with Kevin's help, poor old Tim would have a hard time making it as a human. He couldn't read or write and had little idea of how to act with other people. And yet he was brave and faithful and good. Kevin shrank at the thought that in time, Tim might grow to be ashamed of himself.

With a suppressed groan, Kevin turned the flashlight off and lay down again. How did I get mixed up in all this? he asked himself. I have enough troubles of my own to handle. And they're only going to get worse if we go back home like this. I wonder if parents ever split up because they can't agree on which insane asylum is best for their kid?

The velvety darkness inside the tent had a soothing effect on Kevin. He placed his arms under his head, staring blankly into space. A blur of images began to swirl before his eyes and slowly the extraordinary events of the past two days began to replay in his mind, like a documentary taped for TV.

The morning of the camp-out had begun well. He'd managed to get permission for Tim to come along without much trouble. The weather had been great, and the new tan pop-tent Dad gave him for his birthday had set up easy as a breeze. It was right after the tent was up that things had started to go wrong. First Tim chased the rabbit into the woods, then they'd gotten lost, and then they'd stumbled on that rotten pond! At this point, realizing that he was getting to the important part, Kevin shifted his memory into slow motion.

He could see himself and Tim as they first entered the clearing by the pond—hot, thirsty, and tired. Almost at once he'd tripped over something in the grass. Yes, it was that old wooden board shaped like a thick arrow.

CHANGEWATER POND, it had said, sort of like a road sign telling the name of the place.

As he stared into the darkness, that odd name took on a new significance to Kevin. What did it mean—that the pond water appeared to change color with the season? Or that its depth changed when there was a lot of rain? But, wait a minute—maybe it wasn't the water itself that changed, but that it *worked* a change . . . upon whatever went into it!

Kevin's mind freeze-framed that idea while he examined it. That had to be it! The name on the sign was a warning, and it meant that the water would work a change on creatures that went into it. Hadn't he seen that himself? Hadn't Tim changed right before his eyes!

And now, excitedly unreeling his memory further, Kevin remembered something else that he'd scarcely noticed at the time. He saw again the little red-eyed salamander that had slipped into the water, been swamped by a huge ripple, and then suddenly was replaced by a shiny green frog like the one on the shore. That salamander had changed just as Tim had!

With a cry of glee, Kevin reached out to pound his companion into wakefulness. Then his hand fell back. If it was as simple as that—just a dunk in the pond—why hadn't Tim changed back to being a dog again that very day? He'd jumped in and out of the water about twenty times. There had to be something he'd overlooked.

Kevin forced his tired brain back over the events of that day at the pond. Wel-l, go back to the sign. Uh-huh! Something besides the name was written on it. Some silly little slogan in fading letters . . . but what was it? . . . What? He tried to zero in on the writing but couldn't. He was just too tired. Tomorrow morning, he resolved, they would get up early and try to find Changewater Pond once again.

As he was drifting off to sleep, an optimistic little voice in Kevin's head reminded him to tell Tim everything he'd learned about how to win at the dog obedience trials *before* they started to experiment again. And then a pessimistic little voice warned him that if nothing worked out, he'd better pack up Tim and the tent and make tracks for California.

·∙੩ 9 ੬∙·

Why are ye starin' at me like that so early in the morning?" asked Tim, awakening to find Kevin kneeling beside him. "Have I sprouted flowers out of me navel or somethin'?"

Kevin laughed and thumped Tim's air mattress. "With you, Tim, it could happen. Actually, I was just trying to remember all the things I want to tell you this morning before we take another shot at transforming you back to a dog."

"Yahoo!" Tim sat bolt upright. "I knew

ye'd think of something after a good night's sleep. What are we doing? Where are we going? Tell me about it!"

"I think we should go back to Changewater Pond, Tim. We've only been wasting time around here. Last night I had a few ideas, but—oh, there's no sense talking about it until we get there."

"We can eat first, can't we, Kevin?" asked Tim anxiously. At Kevin's nod he went out to lovingly survey their larder.

Kevin dressed quickly and followed him outside. There, Tim handed him a newly created culinary masterpiece—a banana spread thickly with peanut butter and studded with raisins. As they ate, Kevin eyed his companion thoughtfully. Now, while Tim was still human and could understand words clearly, he should explain all about the dog obedience routines. But at the same time, he'd have to be careful not to insult him about his former mistakes.

"Tim," he said slowly, "I want to pass along some tips I've learned from Aunt Fiona about show dogs. She talks about you all the time—what you're doing and how well you work."

"She *does?*" Tim was all ears.

"You bet! Just for starters, Aunt Fiona says that you are the best and most beautiful and smartest Irish setter in the whole world. She expects that you'll be the first Redlightning super champion in a long line of blue-ribbon winners."

"I will?"

"Yep. Only there's one problem. She says that sometimes you're too smart for your own good."

"*Too* smart—yeah, that sounds like me," Tim admitted, blushing happily. "Er, what d'ye actually mean by that?"

Kevin relaxed. Flattery, he was discovering, worked wonders. Now it wasn't so difficult to explain to Tim that sometimes he acted too quickly and without considering Fiona's wishes, that his job was not to lead Fiona around and outguess the judges, but that they were out there as partners.

"So you see, Tim," he finished, "it's teamwork that counts. Each of you has to work closely with the other, like members of a squad or a family. . . . Well, the way a family *should* work together."

Tim didn't seem to notice Kevin's voice trail off thoughtfully. Jumping to his feet, he cried, "C'mon, let's get back to that pond right away."

Kevin grabbed the knapsack and they set out across the wide field once again.

At the edge of the woods, Kevin paused uncertainly. "Okay, Tim, it's your turn to show your stuff," he said. "I hope you haven't lost your sense of smell, because I don't know how else we'll find our way from here."

Tim pulled anxiously at his nose. Then he brightened. "A good nose can surely help, but lately I've been learnin' to sharpen up me eyesight, too. You've probably been doin' that all your life, right, Kevin?"

"Maybe, but I wish I'd looked around more carefully when we were here before. Hey, let's pool our talents. If we combine your dog's technique of using the ears and nose, *and* our human eyesight, we should be a terrific pair! Let's try it."

And to Tim's delight, Kevin cocked his head to one side like a curious puppy and listened. Then he raised his head to sniff the breeze. He turned to Tim. "Amazing! I never really noticed how noisy bumblebees are—or how strong the wild clover smells."

Now it was Tim's turn. With great dignity he shaded his eyes with one hand and slowly surveyed the view in all directions. "My excellent eyeballs tell me," he pronounced in a deep voice, "that we are now in a field!"

"A brilliant deduction, oh wise one! But we'd better not waste any more time."

They walked slowly and observed with care. Eventually a pattern of crushed plants, dislodged stones, and a bit of blue denim thread dangling from a bush indicated that they had found their own trail. Once, Tim exclaimed loudly and pinched his nose together with his fingers, claiming to have picked up the scent of Kevin's much worn sneakers.

As the woodland thickened, the novelty

wore off. "I'd have found the pond long ago if only I were me proper self again," Tim moaned impatiently.

Kevin, a few feet ahead of him, exclaimed and pointed to a series of footprints smeared across a flat rock. "That's dried *mud*, Tim. If we were still carrying mud on our feet at this point two days ago, we must be close to water!"

In a burst of speed, they emerged together into the little clearing and again saw the pond directly in front of them. Without a moment's hesitation, Tim ran headlong down the slope, shedding his scorned human clothing as he went. Kevin followed more slowly. A strange, hollow feeling was spreading inside him. This might, he realized, be the last time he saw his redheaded friend as he now appeared. He'd miss him.

The pond below them appeared calm, waiting even. Before Kevin got there, Tim launched his body into a dive—flat out, like the first time. Like the first time the water smacked against his stomach with a loud report. And, like all the other times, he emerged a boy.

Tears of frustration misted his eyes as he crawled, dripping, onto the bank. "Oh, Kevin," he said, "I really thought it would work this time. Why didn't anything *happen?*"

Kevin crouched beside him, his mind a muddle of relief, annoyance, and sympathy. "Remember our talk this morning about working as a team?" he asked. "Well, we're still a couple of klutzes, Tim. *You* dashed off just now without waiting to find out what I had in mind. And *I* didn't tell you what I'd figured out last night about the Changewater Pond sign. I'm sure now that the short slogan-thing written beside the name will clue us in on what to do next."

Tim heaved an impatient sigh and they both began to search the grass near the edge of the woods. Although Kevin kept his fingers crossed on both hands, it was Tim who found the sign lying face down, as they had left it.

Holding the muddy post upright, Kevin

squinted at the faint, spidery writing on the boards. He read aloud, "CHANGEWATER POND . . . that's the part I remembered last night, Tim. Here's the part I forgot. It says, WHAT YOU SEE IS WHAT YOU GET!" He paused and burst out angrily, "So, of *course* whatever you see is what you're going to get. This cruddy thing doesn't help a bit!" Disgustedly he shoved the heavy sign at Tim.

"Well," said Tim, looking it over grimly, "the only thing I *see* here is a stupid ignoramus of a board—and that is what I am going to get *rid* of!" He grasped the sign and with a heave, tore it off the decaying post. There was a satisfying screech of rusty nails. "And now I'm going to smash it into a million pieces and drown it for refusing to give us a clue!"

The sight of Tim striding furiously through the grass with his awkward burden made Kevin grin in spite of his frustration.

With total concentration, Tim knelt beside the pond and battered at the board with a large rock, then he sank the pieces in the shallow water and trampled them into the mud.

At last, his anger spent, he dropped dejectedly among the reeds, staring at the flat and secretive waters.

Kevin was on his way to join him when suddenly Tim leaped to his feet.

"Did you see that, Kevin, did you see that?" he shouted hoarsely, pointing into the pond. "It's all a *lie*! Nothing works like it should. There are no changes anymore."

"What? Did I see what? What are you talking about?" Kevin shook Tim's shoulder roughly.

With an effort, Tim calmed down enough to explain himself. "Well, as I was sitting there, some little black . . . bugs came down the bank and one fell in the water. And when it came back up again, it was *still the same*! Like I am. See? The pond doesn't change things, Kevin."

"But, Tim, it changed you the first time. And you weren't the only one either. Do you remember that red-eyed salamander? Well, it changed into a frog—only I didn't realize that until last night." Kevin paused and forced a tone of confidence into his voice. "Tell me every little detail you remember about those bugs, Tim. We must be overlooking something important."

"Okay," Tim said trustfully. "I was just sitting there in the weeds, sort of staring into space, when three or four little black bugs, ants, I guess they were, came marching down the path one behind the other. You know how they do that?"

"Yeah, I know how they walk along single file, like on an invisible pathway. Go on."

"Well, when the first one got to the edge of the pond, it kept right on going, out onto some soggy little leaves. Not too smart, y'see. They sank, and the ant fell in the water. I was holding my breath, Kevin, so I wouldn't disturb what was happening. But—when the ant came up out of the water, it was the same as it had been before!"

"What about the other ants? Did they fall in, too?"

"No. They stopped at the edge. They seemed, like, worried at what happened to the first one, you know? They kept wiggling their wispy feeler things in the air, sort of signaling to it. As soon as it crawled out, they all went off again, single file."

"So, let's see. There've been three kinds of dunkings into that pond—you, the salamander, and the ant," mused Kevin. "But the only transformation I saw clearly was yours."

"Yeah," broke in Tim. "The first thing *I* saw when I came up out of the water was your scared-lookin' face."

"And earlier," cried Kevin with rising excitement, "when the salamander surfaced, the only creature he could have seen was that frog croaking on the rock. So he became a frog! That's the secret, Tim—that's how Changewater Pond works! Like the sign says, 'What you see is what you get'!"

"I still don't understand, Kevin," wailed Tim. "How come the ant never changed but the others did!"

Kevin knit his brows. "Look, Tim, you were a dog when you jumped into the magic pond. A dog saw a boy when he first came up out of the water and changed to a boy. A salamander saw a frog and changed to a frog. But the ant saw another ant, so it remained an ant. And the reason that you didn't change to a dog again today is that you are now a boy—and kept seeing me, another boy."

"Oh-h. Is that all there is to it?" asked Tim coolly. "What do we do now?"

"What do we do? Why, we've got to go get ourselves another dog. You've got to see a dog when you poke your head out of the water again. Next time it's going to work!"

Tim's smile split his face from ear to ear. He rushed over to his clothes and yanked them on. "Oh, Kevin," he said breathlessly as the two streaked off into the trees, "ye'll be sure to get us the proper kind of dog, won't ye? I don't want to end up some twit of a little poodle!"

·⋅ᢒ 10 ᢒ⋅·

Kevin and Tim reached the field behind Richie's house as the sun climbed to its noon-time high. A slight breeze was stirring and the nylon walls of Kevin's little tent rippled peace-fully. The two boys stopped briefly to grab apples and some cookies and continued on into town.

"Och, Kevin, what will we do if no one's home at Bridget's house?" asked Tim anxiously as they crossed the town square.

"Y'know what, Tim? I've been thinking

about Bridget. I'm sure this changeover thing will work okay as long as we have another Irish setter. But you *might* turn into a female dog."

Tim shrugged. "So what? I could still be a champion, Kevin," he replied. Then his eyes widened. "Now I see what you mean. Fiona wouldn't believe it was me, and we'd be almost as badly off as we are right this minute. So, scratch Bridget and think of some male setter, Kevin."

Kevin veered off the path and clomped up the wooden steps of the bandstand. He sank onto a bench, clutching his forehead. "Geez, Tim, it isn't that easy. I can't just go sidling up to someone I don't know and ask to use their dog in a little experiment I'm working on." He sighed. "The only other male Irisher I know is crazy old Corky."

"So who's Corky and what's crazy about him?" Tim found a shaded corner and stretched out on the warm boards.

"He belongs to a lady Mom knows, and he's wild. Corky's real big and Mrs. Brown's real little—you should see her trying to walk him. Corky goes charging down the street with her flapping at the other end of the leash like a buffalo tethered to a sparrow."

Tim didn't smile. "Poor Corky," he said. "It sounds like he doesn't get enough exercise. That just makes everything worse." He regarded Kevin curiously. "Are you worried that you won't be able to handle Corky, Kevin?"

"Not anymore. I can tell the difference now between a mean dog and one who's just too full of beans." Kevin stood up. "Okay, let's give old Corkbrain a try."

They clattered back down the steps and changed their direction. The Browns' well-tended Tudor home was several blocks from the center of town, on the street where Kevin lived. As the boys approached, a long white Lincoln Continental appeared, backing slowly out of the driveway. Mrs. Brown's small head was barely level with the top of the steering wheel.

"Mrs. Brown! Hey, wait a minute, Mrs. Brown!" Kevin yelled, breaking into a run.

The white car rolled to a stop and the window opened. Mrs. Brown twittered a greeting to Kevin.

"Oh, I'm fine, Mrs. Brown," he answered breathlessly. "I wanted to ask if I could borrow Corky for a while. I've been exercising my Aunt Fiona's dog for her lately, but they're away now. I really miss the big guy, so I wondered if I could take Corky for a run."

Kevin wished he'd had time to think up a better reason, but as it turned out, there was no need. Mrs. Brown was obviously delighted. "Why, Kevin, Corky will love it!" she said. "Just ring the doorbell and ask Rosa to leash him up for you." The car moved on and then stopped again. "And, Kevin, if Corky gets rambunctious, just give him a stick to carry in his mouth. He loves to chase sticks."

In no time, Kevin found himself being yanked down the driveway by a powerful setter who had no intentions of wasting a minute of this unexpected outing. Tim, who had been waiting patiently back at the sidewalk, now rushed eagerly toward them.

Suddenly Corky stopped short, sniffing the air suspiciously. A low growl rumbled in his throat and the hackles along his spine rose like a punk haircut.

Oh no, what now—a dog fight? thought Kevin, bracing himself for trouble. Then, to his utter astonishment, Corky whined and cowered back against Kevin's legs. No matter how hard Kevin tugged, not one more step would the dog take.

"You've spooked him, Tim!" he cried. "Corky knows there's something weird about you. He won't go near you."

Tim's expression was grim. "Even me own kind don't know me now. I'm like one of those changeling creatures caught betwixt your world and me own." His voice became desperate. "Do something, Kevin! We've got to get him to the pond!"

Kevin knelt and ran his hand along Corky's quivering sides in long, calming strokes. "Tim's okay, boy, don't be afraid. Just relax and he'll explain all this to you later on, okay?"

Corky was not persuaded. And when Kevin went behind him to shove him forward, he dug in with all twenty toenails—immovable as the Rock of Gibraltar.

Just then an airport limousine roared by, heading in the direction of Kevin's house. In the backseat a woman with chestnut-colored hair leaned forward in an animated conversation with the driver.

Tim turned and shrank into the shelter of some shrubs. "That was Fiona, Kevin!" he cried in a horrified voice. "I'd not want her to see me like this. Do you think she noticed us?"

"Nope. But if she's back in town, we only have a few more hours to work with. We'd better separate now and meet again at the pond, Tim. I think Corky will be okay if you're not with us."

Tim agreed, and started off at once. Kevin waited until he'd turned the corner and then set out with Corky. After a few hesitant steps, the dog returned to his old habits, straining against his collar so that each breath was a strangled grunt. Kevin gladly gave him his head, and soon they were racing through the town at breakneck speed.

When at last they crashed through the line of trees that bordered the meadow at Changewater Pond, Kevin could see that Tim was already there. As soon as Corky got wind of him, he skidded to a stop and sank flat on his belly in the grass.

Tim's long, bare legs began to quiver with impatience. "No more foolin' around, Kevin. Just haul ol' Corkbrain up into a squat so I can fasten me eyes on him as soon as I raise me head from the water. Here goes!" he yelled, and dashed off down the slope.

"But, Tim, you'll see us *both* and who knows . . ." Kevin's voice broke off, unheeded. Wouldn't that guy *ever* learn?

At the edge of the pond, however, Tim braked himself abruptly and turned about with an embarrassed smile. "Hey, Kevin," he called, "maybe we'd better get our signals straight before I dive in."

"No kidding, *partner*," said Kevin. "We're never going to get this right unless we work on it together."

"Okay, okay! 'Twas in the back o' me mind all along." Tim's eyes went back to Corky. "It's too bad about this poor devil gettin' spooked, Kevin. I wish you could get him closer to the pond and tell him to sit still for once."

"Fat chance with you around," said Kevin. "We'll have to think of something else."

"Hey, I know! Since he's so scared of me, maybe I can get him downhill another way."

As Kevin waited, puzzled, Tim snaked through the grass in a wide circle behind his friend and the nervous setter. Then he broke from cover and ran toward them, howling like a banshee.

Corky's drooping ears flew straight up in fright. Instead of being driven downhill, he leaped sideways and made for home. At the other end of the leash, Kevin was jerked off his feet, and he crash-landed in one of the huckleberry bushes, finally dragging Corky to a stop.

"You stupid idiot!" Kevin shouted at Tim, unraveling the leash from around his wrist. "Why didn't you tell me what you were up to? I could have been killed!"

"Well, don't get mad, Kevin, you *are* closer to the water." One look at his friend's purple face convinced Tim that this was no time for humor. "Okay, I know what you're goin' to say. I promise I won't make another move without your say-so . . . partner."

Kevin picked absently at the twigs tangled in his hair. "Um-m-m, maybe we can *trick* this ornery beast into helping us," he said at last.

"Trick him?" Tim gazed at Kevin admiringly. "How are we going to do that?"

"Okay. First of all, you walk quietly down to the pond and wait—motionless. I'll prop Corky upright next to this big huckleberry bush. When we're in the right position, I'll signal by raising one hand. You dive into the water, and just when you begin to surface, I'll leave Corkbrain and duck behind the bush. That way, when you come up, you'll see only him. How's that sound?"

It sounded a lot better than it worked out. Corky was so nervous that the moment Kevin moved away, he dove for cover, too. Much to Kevin's disgust they both ended up in the huckleberry bush.

After an anxious look at the sun, now arching down the sky, Tim promptly lost all compassion for his fellow setter. "Let's *stake* him into position," he said savagely. He fished out a dripping piece of the old sign he'd broken earlier and waved it at Kevin. "I'll get the wooden post for this thing and hammer it into the ground. Then we tie Corky to it nice and tight, okay?"

At Kevin's nod he started up the bank, tossing the piece of broken board back into the water. That was a mistake. Chasing sticks was Corky's major passion. With a powerful lunge he tore out of Kevin's grasp and raced toward the pond.

"Oh no!" shrieked Kevin. "Not another dog-boy! Grab him, Tim, before he hits that water!"

What happened next, Kevin would always remember but never quite believe. The incredible Timothy leaped forward, and with a body block that would credit a professional football lineman, he intercepted Corky in midair. The two met with such force that although the dog was knocked aside onto the grassy banks, Tim ricocheted backward into the pond.

Kevin had just enough presence of mind left to throw himself out of sight behind the huckleberry bushes.

The waters of Changewater Pond roiled and bubbled as if in the throes of a storm. From beneath the churning currents rose a thatch of auburn hair and two brown eyes that fixed themselves on the stunned figure of Corky, still gasping on the bank. It sank once again. Then, amid the turmoil a sleek head broke the surface and its owner swam swiftly to shore.

With a shout of exultation, Kevin crashed out of the bushes and threw his arms around the joyfully wriggling, all-dog, all-Irisher Redlightning Timothy.

·◦) 11 (◦·

Autumn had come early this year. Kevin shivered as he mounted the broad front steps to his house. Already there was a bite to the air and the neat piles of leaves he'd raked from under the sugar maples were brilliant with splashes of scarlet and yellow.

He unlocked the door and stared gloomily into the silent hallway. No one was home, of course. The mail lay scattered over the floor beneath the slot in the door. Kevin's mood lifted—maybe there'd be another letter from Fiona.

He scooped up the small drift of envelopes

and riffled through them as he walked into the kitchen. No luck. Disappointed, Kevin poured himself a glass of cold milk and stacked a generous supply of graham crackers on the table in front of him. Almost without thinking, he reached into his back pocket and withdrew a well-worn blue envelope. It was dated two weeks earlier.

Dear Folks, and especially Kevy:

Our circuit of dog shows is almost finished now—only two more to go. Tim and I are having a wonderful time and working together better than ever. He's picked up two show ribbons and is making progress in the novice obedience trials, too. I can scarcely believe how much he's matured over the summer. He's attentive and cooperative, yet so full of spirit that the crowds fall in love with him. He waves that magnificent tail of his and it's as if he's saying, "This is my job, folks, and I love it!" Do you know what I mean, Kevy? Maybe that weekend of just pure fun while camping out with you relaxed him or something.

And now for my really big news—which won't

surprise you, sister Kate. That certain young veterinarian did decide to become a partner in my kennel, and I did agree to become his wife. Yes, really! I'll tell you more when we get back to New Hampshire.

Love to you all,
Fiona and Tim

Kevin knew the contents of the letter so well by now that he didn't need to read it. Just looking at it made him feel happy. It made him dare to believe that his adventure with Tim had really happened.

A clamor from the telephone interrupted his thoughts. It was his mother. "Hi, Kev, I'm so glad you're home early today," she said. "Fiona just called me at the office and as usual she's in a rush. She and Tim will arrive this afternoon and fly back to Dublin in the morning. She's gotten a part-time job at the animal quarantine station and also needs to make wedding arrangements. And Kevin, Fiona is bringing a surprise for you."

He took a sharp breath. "Is it a silver cup? Could Tim possibly have won the top prize, Mom?"

118

"You really couldn't expect that yet, Kevin. But I think you'll like this surprise just as well. No more questions, m'lad! We're all trying to keep it a secret until she gets here. In the meantime, can you make a run to the food market for me? You've been such a help lately, I hate to ask you again so soon."

Kevin said that he didn't mind, and pulled over the yellow pad and a pencil. Despite the lengthening grocery list, his smile grew broader and broader. When his mother finally hung up, he exploded into a whoop of joy.

"Tonight!" he shouted to his reflection in the hall mirror as he pulled on his jacket. "They're coming tonight!" Then the face before him sobered. "Too bad they can't stay longer. Tim and I won't even have time to hunt for Changewater Pond." As he turned away, he thought again how strange it was that he'd never been able to find that pond again—not even when he and Richie had taken Corky along with them.

Much to everyone's pleased surprise, Fiona arrived on time for dinner that evening. The rented station wagon, now dusty from her long trip, sped up the driveway just as Mr. Mason was placing the glass salad bowl on the table.

Kevin was down the steps in a flash and reached the car even before the driver's door was fully open.

"Hi, Kevin, love," cried his aunt, slipping out and enveloping him in a bear hug. "I have *so* much to tell. . . ." Their greetings were cut short by eager yelps from the back of the car, where Tim was pawing at the hatch. As Fiona went around to unlock it, Kevin positioned himself in a solid wrestler's stance. He threw his arms out wide and called, "Yo, Tim! Get over here, you crazy nut!"

No encouragement was necessary. Tim exploded out of the car like an eighty-pound rocket, hurtling straight for Kevin. They hit the grass in a tangle. Boy and dog rolled over and over with ecstatic whines and shouts of laughter.

The three adults watched this wild welcoming scene with conspiratorial smiles on their faces. "Good lord," exclaimed Mr. Mason, "how that boy has changed. Six months ago he hardly knew a dog from a lawn mower—and now, well, he's pretty good with both."

Fiona nodded. "He's ready," she said. Raising two fingers to her lips, she whistled sharply to the two on the lawn. "Okay, me lads. Now let's take a look at the big surprise, eh?"

The wrestlers rose immediately and followed her to the back of the car, where she pulled forward Tim's traveling cage. From a cozy nest of blankets, Fiona gently lifted a ball of fluffy tan fur, which she placed flat against Kevin's chest. He clutched it instinctively, and at once the puppy nuzzled its way upward and licked him lightly, trustingly, under the chin.

"Oh, Aunt Fiona!" cried Kevin. "Is it for *me*?" The bright colors of the autumn day blurred and he buried his face against the warm, downy-soft little body in his arms.

"Oh, but . . ." He looked anxiously toward his parents.

His mother and father were standing close together, and he saw by their smiles that no appeal was needed. They'd all been in on this surprise together!

"Yes, Kev, she's all yours," said his mother gently. "We know you'll take good care of her."

"Your mother and I decided that Redlightning Timothy there wasn't the only one who grew up a lot over the last summer," his father added.

The adults mounted the stairs to sit in the wicker porch chairs, but Kevin settled happily on the bottom step with the curious pup nibbling at his earlobe. He whistled to Tim, but the big dog seemed to have other ideas. He had squeezed among the adults and was pressing his muzzle in Fiona's hand.

Fiona looked down fondly. "Don't fret, Tim. I'll be tellin' all about your part in this right away." She turned to her nephew solemnly. "I want you to know, Kevin Mason, that Timothy himself chose this pup for you. Believe me, lad, Tim is one unusual animal!"

Kevin's heart swelled with happiness. "Oh, I do believe it, Aunt Fiona. No one in the world knows better than I just *how* unusual Timothy really is!"

His mother gave him a searching look, but Fiona had already launched into her story. "So-o, there we were on a lovely sunny afternoon—just Tim and me and a litter of ten Irish setter pups scramblin' about in an outdoor pen. Each one was more darlin' than the next and I was in a perfect dither of indecision. While I handled them, Tim sat motionless beside me, like he was holding his breath. And then he stretched out his muzzle and nudged this perfect little female over toward me. So insistent he was that the feisty mite actually turned around and nipped his nose with those teeny-tiny milk teeth. That did it. I had to agree that she was the one."

A tight knot of sadness began to loosen inside Kevin. Although Tim was going far away to live with Fiona, he'd managed to choose a new companion for Kevin—all for him this time, to be completely his own. Tim met Kevin's grateful gaze and padded down the steps to sit beside him. Kevin threw one arm across the big dog's silky shoulders and resettled his wriggling pup in the crook of the other. "Thanks, Tim," he said. Then he smiled and leaned closer, whispering, "I hope you've warned her never to jump into any weird-looking ponds!"

And Tim grinned back at him with an expression in his brown eyes that was remarkably intelligent for a dog.